WILDERNESS FAIRIES

A True Story

R. A. PACE

WILDERNESS FAIRIES
A TRUE STORY

iUniverse books may be ordered through booksellers or by contacting:

iUniverse
1663 Liberty Drive
Bloomington, IN 47403
www.iuniverse.com
844-349-9409

ISBN: 978-1-6632-5764-2 (sc)
ISBN: 978-1-6632-5763-5 (e)

Library of Congress Control Number: 2023921382

Print information available on the last page.

iUniverse rev. date: 11/07/2023

Contents

CHAPTER 1

SOMEWHERE IN BETWEEN PACKING up the car and breathing in the fresh mountain air, I came to a place called the Wilderness. But, at this time, there were only two dogs, Jack and Russell. Lily had not been adopted yet. So, on this day, only two dogs and myself went hiking in the very place where this story began.

I took the pack out of the green Subaru, and hooked up Jack and Russell to their leashes. I had lived in England, Germany, and Saudi Arabia so sometimes I called things by a different name. For instance, in 2004, when this chapter took place, I called dog leashes "leads" as they do in England. I had traveled to over fifteen countries but that's a story for another book. I was young, twenty-four, and well-traveled—fortunate enough to see the world as a military woman; seeing museums and historic sites, and eating good food. But nothing compared to seeing the fairies for the first time on that mountain in the middle of the moonstruck night, in 2005 at the age of twenty-five. However, this chapter is about the fairies getting me into trouble, but not bad trouble, just enough trouble to make me realize that strange things do happen.

Jack, Russell, and I began to walk down the Laurel Creek trail in Pisgah National Forest, a wilderness that had been donated by the Vanderbilt family. The trail was not too difficult, simply a dirt and rock trail that had seen better days, eroded and nearly covered with wiry brush and tree limbs. The dogs didn't seem to mind. They barreled through the trail covering without hesitation. Eventually the trail started to dip down, making it difficult for me to stay balanced with two Jack Russell terriers pulling me onward. We came to the creek crossing. The dogs drank some cool mountain water, and I put down my pack, opened it, and drank out of a canister. Mountain water would cause an upset stomach if consumed without being treated. So I drank the processed well water from the house that I was renting out while attending college at Western Carolina University as an undergraduate student.

Finished with a refreshing pit stop, Jack and Russell began to dance around again, waiting for the next leg of the hike. As we walked, I heard the crashing water of a waterfall. Curious, I led Jack and Russell off-trail to what looked like a rocky overlook. However, it was too steep to be reached and the dogs were pulling. So, we turned around and followed the main trail back down, further into the woods. I heard rumbling, like that of a bear, so, with no other option, Jack, Russell, and I took a trail that went deep into the creek's watershed.

"Jack, Russell! This way!" I yelled.

The dogs wagged their tails. We dove deep into the

wilderness, protected by wiry branches that a bear would not be able to climb through.

I ducked down, pushing away the branches from overgrown brush and trees laying lower to the ground and followed Jack, white, and Russell, brown. I loved both dogs. They had been loyal friends who had been there during the worst part of my life. I had wanted to spoil them with a long hike and we were on course to enjoy a summer day. The trail went down, down, down the side of a mountain, and was suddenly covered with dirt and mud. I started to slip because of the dogs pulling.

"Stop!" I cried.

I noticed something strange. The forest suddenly went quiet. All that I could hear was the sound of rushing water. The scene of the forest altered: there was green moss and dampness everywhere. I saw a ring of colorful mushrooms at the base of an old, large tree. While mushrooms are a common sight in the wilderness, these mushrooms were different. They were red with white spots, varying in size, and placed in a perfect ring as if a creature lived near the center. But I kept hiking.

Eventually, I came to the base of the mountains. Laurel Creek was gushing with water hitting rock. I could hear a waterfall but could not see it. I looked across the creek and noticed that hikers had left markers noting that they were lost.

"Oh, great. Jack, Russell, we're apparently lost."

The dogs went to the water's edge. Logic and a good dose of common sense told me to turn around, but the trail was no longer visible, and I knew that hiking out was going to be difficult since the trail that I had followed was overgrown with brush.

"Well, dogs, it's time to rock hop." I laughed.

I knew that following Laurel Creek out would save myself and the dogs from climbing up the mountain and potentially not reaching the main trail that spread out from the parking lot near Sam Knob and Art Loeb's Shining Rock. So, we started to hop from one rock to another. This went on for about ten minutes until I noticed a vole on a rock in the middle of the creek. The poor thing, black and camouflaged from potential predators, was going in circles, desperately trying to avoid being overcome by the rushing water. Apparently, the blind vole had rested on the rock before a rain shower and then got trapped.

"Come here, little one. I'll help you."

I cupped my hands and the vole snuggled up to the heat of my palm. I released the vole on the ground. He scurried away.

"OK, Jack and Russell. It's time to keep going. The sun's setting."

The creek came to a bend, and, finally, I saw the waterfall that I had been hearing. It was gushing white water but wasn't the only waterfall. I could see a series of waterfalls, each easy to climb; which was a relief because the brush at the edge of the fall was so dense that it was nearly as sturdy as a brick wall.

Jack, Russell, and I started to do the only thing left as an option: climb. I placed the dogs at the base of the next waterfall and proceeded to throw my leg up to latch onto the top of the rock that the water was going down. This went on for five or six falls.

I came to the crest of the last fall that was reachable and turned around to see that the sun had almost set completely.

"OK, God. OK."

I took Jack and Russell off their leashes and let them roam. They found an opening in the brush. Like a monkey, I swung through the branches of the brush while Jack and Russell scouted out the next opening. I felt as though I was being watched but couldn't stop. Night was falling and I was scared. An hour later, I came to the main trail. Jack and Russell barked. I was relieved. We walked out of the wilderness the same way we came in, with waterfalls splashing in the distance. At the parking lot, I was no longer frightened. I no longer felt alone. And I felt more connected to my two heroes, Jack and Russell. I knew that all of it had something to do with that circle of mushrooms. Something so simple to believe but evidently true.

CHAPTER 2

THE YEAR IS NOW 2023. I first encountered the fairies, or so I thought, in 2004 while I was attending school. I was studying history and philosophy, both in the European concentration, and both sensible subjects. So, when I saw the toad stool ring, I thought that there was nothing to it, that it was silly to think that fairies lived under mushrooms, held meetings in the center of the ring, or anything of the sort. I was an atheist before that hike. I didn't believe in anything magical or mystical. By 2005, I had become Catholic following my studies of Europe, both in philosophy and in its history. I began to believe in things outside of logical conclusions. What is to follow is so telling of the truth that I think that any way that I write it, it's no more than a reminder. So, before I begin, I should note that, I've decided to tell the story like children's storybooks do. So, here, the real story begins …

CHAPTER 3

ONCE UPON A TIME, there was a young woman, a young woman who had grown up. And with her, there were three dogs, and an aspiration to go hiking. The young woman loved both her dogs, Jack, Russell, and Lily, and a good hike. She never knew of where she would hike next, or whether or not her dogs, the two Jack Russell terriers and a hound mix, would like the trail. However, the young woman and her dogs drove along the Blue Ridge Parkway stopping at every trailhead one summer. Day in and day out, they went on long trails and short trails, difficult trails and easy trails. They were traveling the world on daily adventures; adventures that led them to the wilderness the young woman had passed by one sunny summer day.

The young woman had seen almost all the world's beauty. But on that day, she and her three dogs would begin an adventure that would lead to another; that would lead to the wilderness outside of woods, on the top of a mountain, and in the middle of that moonstruck night when things that no one expects to happen, happen.

The day was hot; the air was heavy with humidity. The dogs were panting and wagging their tails. After pulling off to a sideroad from the Blue Ridge Parkway, the young woman and her three dogs came to a gravel parking lot and noticed a sign. It read: The Wilderness. The young woman smiled. That was precisely where she wanted to be.

Pulling a pack from the car, the young woman hooked up her three dogs to their leashes and began to walk. At first, everything was fine. Then, a rattlesnake emerged from the brush. The dogs were pulled back. The rattlesnake shook its tail as a warning. It just wanted to be left alone.

"Come on, dogs. Let's go!"

The young woman and her dogs resumed the hike.

The hike into the mountains excited the dogs. They got to sniff and see, jump and wiggle; and no more upset rattlesnakes emerged. There was just flowers and fauna, sun and breeze—a perfect summer day.

When the young woman and her three dogs got to the end of the preliminary trail, the dogs yipped with excitement. There was an open field filled with long grass, wildflowers, and Queen Anne's lace. So, one-by-one, the young woman unhooked the dogs' leads. The Jack, Russell, and Lily ran and hopped and rolled around at the base of the mountain called Sam Knob in the best field that they had ever been in.

"Jack! Russell! Lily! Come here. Come on," the young woman called, whistling, as well.

The three dogs returned to the young woman and were once again put on their leads. They were all still hoping for a good hike.

Another sign appeared at the end of the field's trail,

which read "Laurel Creek" and "Sam Knob." This time, the young woman and her three dogs went to the right to follow the trail to Sam Knob, which would lead to the top of the mountain on that fantastic summer's day.

The trail's incline was tough with sharp, steep switchbacks. At one point, steps led to a rocky overlook. The young woman and her three dogs had to climb through the rocky terrain. The young woman grew tired. She kept stepping.

At the curve of the summit, the young woman spotted a large, white quartz boulder, a rock like she had never seen—she knew, then, that the mountain was enchanted. The three dogs began to wiggle with elation. They had come to the top of Sam Knob. Exhausted, the young woman began to scope out a small area of the summit surrounded by brush for the right spot for the tent, a temporary home for a night's rest. Too soft of ground made the young woman seek out another site. The three dogs began to bark. On the other side of Sam Knob there was a perfect place for camping: open, clear, and soft. The young woman and her three dogs did not have to worry about bears or coyotes at that tent site. So, the young woman dropped her pack as the setting sun shined over the Blue Ridge Mountains and began to set up camp, putting the tent up within minutes. The young woman and her three dogs were happy.

With a new, nightly home established, and with dusk disappearing upon the mountains, the young woman and her three dogs nestled in the tent and fell asleep within an hour.

Around midnight, the young woman awoke to her three dogs snoring. She opened the tent flap and gazed at the stars shining down from an open, clear night's sky. Contented, the young woman returned to her sleeping bag, and fell back into a deep sleep, facing a calm that lured her into sweet dreams filled with joy.

A few hours later, the young woman awoke to an unusual silence and unusual stillness. The wind had been whipping around the tent but it suddenly stopped, which sparked curiosity in the young woman. So she opened the tent flap again, and, as her vision cleared, she saw what she thought were lightning bugs just six feet away from the tent; dozens and dozens of lightning bugs. But they weren't. At closer glance, the young woman widened her eyes to see that what she thought to be bugs were little people engrossed in light. *Amazing*, the young woman thought, who had left childhood imagination behind her. The young woman tried to be logical. She thought that there might be a species of lightning bugs unknown to anyone. But the fairies drew near. They were all tiny people lit up without dimming. The fairies danced around in the air right before the young woman. They were perfect creatures. The three dogs didn't wake.

The young woman continued to merely gaze. They were part of nature's beauty: wilderness fairies. In the calm, moonstruck night, a single tear rolled down the young woman's face. She remembered her childhood and seeing

12

the very sight in her dreams. She smiled slowly until the light of the fairies lit up in her eyes and pulled herself back inside the tent. She once again fell into a sleep without nightmares, a sleep during which no bad thing came into her thoughts, no memory of war. No memory of anything awful. The young woman fell asleep to the peaceful fairies' light, an unworldly bliss.

Dawn came. The young woman rose from her sleep. The three dogs shook and shivered with a pleasant joy. They were awake and looking forward to another day. The young woman fed her dogs, and then stood at the edge of the cliff of Sam Knob and smiled again. She remembered little but felt loved.

"Come here, dogs! I love you all equally." The dogs barked as the young woman hugged them all at once. "Silly things. It's time to go back home."

The young woman noticed that there was no sign of what she had seen. She decided to keep it all a secret. Awake and ready, the young woman and her dogs walked down and back again to the base of the mountain. When everyone got back to the car, the young woman laughed with admiration. The wilderness and its fairies had most certainly brought the young woman a lesson about happiness and love. She was grateful.

The End

It is 2023. I haven't seen the fairies over a decade. But, children, I did see them again.

13

CHAPTER 4

THE WORLD HAD ERUPTED in conflict. I took daily walks around the YMCA in Marion, North Carolina, to relieve stress from the feeling that the long wars would never end and that I would once again play some part in perpetuating human discord. So, as it was, I took a walk on the eve of dusk, hoping to also spar weight loss. You see, I was now in my late thirties. I should have had custody of my children but didn't. I had gotten into debt and had no money to adopt my beautiful children who I had been raising as a surrogate. The stepfather was evil. He had been abusive toward the children. So much so that they were in foster care. My life had become complex. Much too complex for a children's story about fairies. But it was the fairies who taught me how to love again, and I love my children with my whole heart. Their real father had died during the war. I needed my little friends. It goes without saying that I was once again in pain. I walked with my head low, hoping for a miracle to end what had become sadness, a grief that was killing my heart. It's not as though I was wanting. But I was poor. I lived in a trailer with my parents whom I paid rent to. I ate simple meals and never shopped for clothes that were new. I had no one. I had drifted far from the days of long walks with my dogs. All three dogs—Jack, Russell, and Lily—were now deceased. Many mistakes had been made, and I was depressed. But in the middle of my walk at the base of the trail around the Y, I heard something. It sounded like a child screaming. I looked up and thought that I was seeing a flying praying mantis. It wasn't. The creature had two small hands with five fingers and a face like a human's, but she was green and hardly had legs. I realized that the fairies had not forgotten me. What I was seeing was a woodland fairy. I couldn't laugh or cry, I was merely stunned. The fairy flew horizontally into the woods and disappeared. A woodland fairy! During the worst time of my life, I remembered the joy of seeing the fairies before. I was once again content. I laughed and smiled, leaving the wood's trail for the parking lot. Going home without saying a word, once again.

CHAPTER 5

I FELT UNBELIEVABLY ALONE. The sun and the moon were both in the early morning sky dawning on the Kingdom of Saudi Arabia. F-15s kept flying toward Iraq, just outside of Baghdad. I couldn't seem to connect to anyone or anything. Mental illness was setting in. Everyone had become so extraordinarily cruel.

I left the trailer for my break, sat down, and noticed my only friend, a bird. He greeted me every morning for a piece of my plain bagel that I got from the chow hall around midnight. He hopped close to me, took the bagel piece and fled. I got up and headed toward the restroom where ants were busy trying to build an underground kingdom.

"Here you go." I took the tobacco from a cigarette and placed it right at their kingdom's entry. They had carried it for about six feet.

Apart from my fellow sentient beings, I sat back down to try to recall any sense of love left in the world. There had been the bird in England when I was stationed there. I was on a castle tour with a man who was violent toward anything gentle. The finch came right up to me, as if to comfort me, and then flew away. And there was the groundhog and dormouse that I was able to save from drunken GIs. There seemed to be so much hate in the world that I couldn't change. Brick and mortar covered all the world's beauty. Something that I encountered all over Europe, Africa, and the Middle East: countries that had succumbed to industrialization and the development of the world. Only paintings now showed a time when concrete had not filled the world, a time when people lived in harmony with the planet. I finished my coffee while watching the moon set below the horizon and the sun overcame the whole of the desert, and went inside to avoid scorching temperatures.

CHAPTER 6

FOLLOWING THE SECOND SIGHTING of another species of fairy, I felt elated. I remembered that infamous night on Sam Knob and began to wonder why the fairies had chosen me. I had always felt connected to nature, but never imagined that I would truly encounter wilderness and woodland fairies. There would be a third sighting. And it would take a fourth for me to truly understand the predicament I was in. I was content to keep the first and second sightings to myself to honor the privacy of the fairies, never even writing about the toadstool ring. But it became evident that the fairies wanted me to write about them for the purpose of heralding the natural world.

CHAPTER 7

IT WAS A BRISK afternoon and a perfect time to walk. I had lost Jack, Russell, and Lily. It had been years since I had any pets at all. So, every day I walked without any friends. I kept up a fast pace, came around the corner of the trail at the YMCA in Marion, North Carolina, and felt something strange. It was a woodland fairy pulling on strands of my hair. She was tiny, blue, and very vivacious. I smiled, kept walking, and decided to ignore her as she flew back into the woods that had been left standing. I could hear little screams like violent singing. I had assumed that the fairies liked me because I was a vegetarian and environmentally friendly. But, as it was, I didn't know why they had chosen me. I just knew that the following day, at the top of the hill at the Y's trail, the fairies didn't come up to me, but were screaming with anger. I had eaten meat. They were devastated. I was no longer getting enough protein from being a vegetarian due to poverty, so I occasionally ate chicken or fish. The fairies were furious. But there was something else that was strange about their plea. Before the catastrophes around the world due to climate change, the fairies were warning me. Their woodlands and wilderness were dying. The land was being exploited for real estate and resources and they were crying for help. And, children, I did the worst thing possible: I didn't write about the fairies. I wrote about politics and forgot about the fairies.

CHAPTER 8

IT'S 2023 ONCE AGAIN. I had long forgotten about the fairies, too busy with work and life. However, Scarlett, a giant schnauzer I adopted, and I went for a ride along the Blue Ridge Parkway one crisp, winter afternoon. We went through what seemed like endless tunnels but finally came to the Pisgah National Forest where I used to take Jack, Russell, and Lily. I turned into a parking lot with sparsely parked cars and began to walk with Scarlett toward the trail that I had been on so many years ago. I stopped for photographs of the Blue Ridge Mountains and eventually came to a part of the trail that split. One side went left; the other side went right. I chose the right side.

Walking briskly, trying to catch my breath, I focused on looking down at the roots so that I wouldn't trip and fall. Scarlett stopped. I looked up. It was a tunnel made from branches and trees. The air was quiet. Scarlett didn't want to go any further. I didn't either. I had lost my imagination and curiosity and I had forgotten about the fairies but, children, I now know writing this that they are still there, woven into the landscape of those mountains.

CHAPTER 9

WIND BLEW THROUGH THE trees of the Backwoods Mountain Historic Trail in Paddy's Creek of Lake James State Park in Nebo, North Carolina. I was with Scarlett, hiking a short distance to get exercise that she so desperately needed. I paused and let the wind blow through my excessively long hair. I knew that it was time. The trees told me that I wasn't an animal, that I needed to connect to people, to live again, to write this. I remembered the fairies soothing me. This time it was the song of the forest.

CHAPTER 10

I<small>N A DEEP SLEEP</small>, I dreamt of fairies and the forests that I had visited on long hikes, short hikes, where I had enjoyed the peace of a calming breeze. Then, suddenly, my mind drifted, but came back to an image of a woman coming out of the ground, into the trees, and then flowering into all the colors of the woods: blue, green, red, yellow, etc. She said,

"I am the spirit of the forest."

I saw the fairies dancing around her in a joyous circle. Amazed, I wondered why the spirit of the forest visited me at the middle age of my life. Was I supposed to save the forest? Perhaps write about the wilderness for all ages to enjoy and remember before it's too late? I went back into a deep sleep. The following morning, I knew what I had to do: scout out the trails where I thought that the fairies might still be. I needed answers.

CHAPTER 11

CC, MY MOTHER'S BLACK standard American poodle, and Scarlett, my black giant schnauzer, stood, sniffing, on the bridge to the hiking trail where the trees spoke to me through the breeze and rustling leaves. The day was hot. However, the dogs didn't seem to mind.

We came to the trailhead, which read: Overmountain Victory National Trail. It was a trail in Lake James State Park's Paddy's Creek area. CC and Scarlett were chomping at the bit to go ahead and start the hike.

The dogs saddled up, side by side, as I hiked in search of any sign of fairies. The sun beat through canopy of the forest onto the gravel ground. CC stopped. It looked as though she had caught sight of something in the brush. Scarlett turned her head, looking confused. Alas, after a few more steps the dogs let me know that nothing was there and that we needed to resume the hike.

Amid the ferns, Scarlett pointed to where she thought that the fairies could be. As my hiking boots cracked against the pine needles below, I anticipated scaring them off. Perhaps Scarlett scared them. I looked, peering around to no avail. CC caught up with Scarlett and we continued up the trail where the forest got darker as the trees grew thicker. Scarlett ran ahead. Nothing. No sign of the fairies emerged.

Only a spider's web with a large green spider blocking the trail. We turned back. The fairies clearly didn't want to be bothered.

As we went back to the car, I gazed out at where the creek met Lake James. Was I looking too hard? Why wouldn't the fairies reappear? CC, Scarlett, and I stopped at the Shortoff Mountain overlook. Did I have to climb that high to see them again? I didn't know. I only took in the sight of the pasture, the horizon of trees meeting the sky, the mountains in blue, and sighed.

CHAPTER 12

DAY TWO OF THE Overmountain Victory Historic Trail—
the other way. I was determined. This time, I only took
Scarlett.

The paved road came out before us, heading toward the
bridge over Paddy's Creek. We crossed the road and Scarlett
charged ahead on the pavement that met the wood plank
of the footpath bridge. We crossed the bridge and came to
the gravel path down to the trail, with the hot sun beating
down on us. Scarlett pointed into the woods. I knew that
this was where the fairies had to be.

Scarlett and I hiked in, and a sign emerged; something
about dogs being kept on a leash. We hiked on. A beautiful
gravel trail appeared. We hiked on again. We came to a bend
and the forest darkened once again due to the heavy foliage.
Moss, ferns, and brush covered the basin of the woodland
trail. Dead leaves seemingly covered everything and dead
gum tree seeds peppered the ground. Scarlett pulled out to
the front. The shadows of the forest were pronounced now
with sunshine peering through. The trail climbed higher
as we walked on a level trail. We came to a white triangle
marker. I looked for any signs of the fairies. There were none,
yet. The sun speckled onto the forest's floor. Scarlett waited
for me to take pictures of the forest. Ferns were everywhere.

Scarlett sniffed. No sign of fairies. Cobblestone hurt my already sore feet. The trail bent left, then straightened to where roots were edging onto the trail. The green turned dark again as the clouds covered the sun. I could hear water. Scarlett, with her hiking vest on, pulled. The sun came back out and then disappeared again. Water trickled over rocks in Paddy's Creek. Still no sign of the fairies. The creek went far beyond sight. Scarlett insisted on following the trail, not giving up, and that there was life in the forest. I saw banana-shaped leaves, bark, moss, shadows, and the clarity. Scarlett stopped to the left, then to the middle, and then behind me. Could it be that something in the forest was scaring them? Bulging roots appeared again, ferns, and maples. Then a seat to sit on in the most peculiar forest. Two wood planks on the bottom and back. I sat down. A blank board peered out before me that once had information about the trail, now unkept. I looked to the left, down the trail, and to the right. Had the fairies all left? Was I not looking in the right place? I had found them on a footpath. I knew that they weren't afraid. So I decided to keep trying. Maybe I was trying too hard again. Perhaps trying to enjoy the hike would lead to them.

Chapter 13

I HAD A DREAM that the fairies would remember me if only I tried one more time to seek them out. So, I packed up the car and headed west to the Blue Ridge Parkway. Scarlett and I came to Buck Springs Overlook. I knew that the trail just beyond the overlook was magical. We walked to the trailhead where stone steps painted brown and green and splashed with sun went up to the top of the trail that curved into the mountain. Rocks and moss lined the trail. Scarlett smelled everywhere in the hope of hunting out a small, probably furry, creature to chase.

At the summit, there was a long trail made of rocky gravel that cracked beneath my hiking boots. The trees embraced the sky and kept the fauna below cool, shaded from the sun. Then came more steps, this time wood timbers. Sand, gravel, and moss paved the ground. The forest's ceiling opened to allow more sunlight below. Scarlett paused for a picture, and we walked on.

Mountain rock bathed the next part of the trail, seemingly bubbling up from the center of the mountain. I carefully walked on the stone while being pulled by Scarlett.

"Slow down, Scarlett!" I exclaimed.

She didn't. She was just as excited to find the fairies as I was.

When we finally made it to a clearing with three seats positioned in a semi-circle, I remembered my youth and the thrill of seeing the Blue Ridge Mountains for the first time. I remembered the sky and clouds and the blue haze, the fairies who enchanted me after I came home from my stint in the war only to be forced to fight from home because the war came to the United States, and even to western North Carolina. All the sadness and loss disappeared. I looked at the mountain and sighed with relief. I was content, even elated, again.

My life had changed forever because of the fairies.

Scarlett and I continued toward their abode. The latter part of the trail snaked out in front of us. We walked forward. The trail grew sparser. I came upon another seat and a spruce pine with a keen outlook to keep the heart inspired. Scarlett and I kept pressing on. Rhododendrons exploded on the trail. We came to what used to be a fork in the trail. Right led to the fairies' home. As we hiked on, I realized that the trail to the fairies that used to be a cave of trees bent over to protect them had been cut off by park rangers. Someone had known to close the trail to protect them. So there were no fairies to be found. The unexpected had happened, but I didn't give up hope. I had the comfort of the mountains, after all. Scarlett and I turned back, got into the car, and drove home. I still wondered if I would ever see the fairies again.

CHAPTER 14

ON A ROUTINE TRIP to the grocery store, sometime after the Buck Springs hike, I had Scarlett in the car. She was excited as always to go on a ride. I was listening to music and enjoying driving through the meadows on the way to the town. In a flash, it happened.

"Ahhh, I just saw a fairy!" I said.

This time, the fairy was a bright blue color with larger wings and an inch-long body. At first, those who enjoy the existence of fairies would say that it was an indigo bunting. It wasn't. She was graceful like a butterfly, floating over the car's windshield. Tiny fairies were following her.

It happened again. I was determined to find my fairy friends in their habitat all along and they found me. I had to thank them. I had to write about them. I had proof of them. I had to write about them to protect the wild, the wilderness, the woodlands, and now, the meadows. Children, all of this is most certainly true. If you're reading this, just know that you are loved by them, that they are real. This story is coming to an end, but you can most surely write your own.

CHAPTER 15

AFTER SEEING WHAT I realized later was a fairy queen accompanied by tiny fairies riding June bugs, I recalled a hike that I took nearly five years before. I had fallen ill. I was no longer able to hike down into the Linville Gorge where my first encounter with the true beauty of the environment began. Where I had first really seen the mountains. But you can. I know that the majesty of the mountains is there. I know that on all these trails, you can find the fairies if you are only willing to. It doesn't always take an elaborate hike. Sometimes it's just a walk with a loved one or a ride through meadows and farmland. Just try. Try to be a good patron of wherever you live. Love the wilderness, woodlands, meadows, or desert in your heart and the fairies will emerge. And, with that, I leave you and I truly hope that you too will see what I have seen in my dreams and have been blessed to see in reality.

Printed in the United States
by Baker & Taylor Publisher Services